Does God Have a Job?
© 2005 by Jeannie St. John Taylor

Published by Kregel Kidzone, an imprint of Kregel
Publications, Grand Rapids, Michigan 49501 USA. All
rights reserved.

Scripture quotations are taken from the *Holy Bible,
New Living Translation,* copyright © 1996. Used by
permission of Tyndale House Publishers, Inc., Wheaton,
IL 60189 USA. All rights reserved.

ISBN 0-8254-3713-X

Printed in China

To
Stanley Baldwin

"Daddy, does God have a job?"
"Oh, yes. Jesus said his Father never stops working."

"God is an engineer. He designed the whole universe. He planned for the sun to shine by day and the moon and stars by night. He decided how high the mountains should rise and how deep to scoop out the sea. He told the oceans not to go beyond their borders. And he did it all for you."

"God is a landlord. He owns the whole world. The mountains, oceans, deserts, and cities belong to him. He watches over the earth to provide a good place for you to live."

"God is a teacher. He is smarter than anyone on earth.
If you listen, he will whisper thoughts that
teach you right from wrong."

My child,
listen to me and
treasure my instructions.
Prov. 2:1

"God is a writer. He wrote down every single day of your life before you were born."

"God is a soldier. He commands an army made up of millions and millions of angels who watch over you."

**"God is a mathematician.
He numbers every hair on your head."**

"God is a farmer. He sends rain and tells the sun to shine so the earth can grow food for animals . . . and for you."

"God is a doctor. He heals your bruises and cuts. If you get so sick that no doctor on earth knows how to help you, God can still heal you."

"God is an artist. He colors the trees green, makes the waters blue, and paints the sky with orange and pink clouds to remind you to think about him."

"God is a shepherd. He guides you in the right way to go while he watches over you and protects you."

"God is a king. He rules over all the kings who ever lived. He appoints leaders who will keep your country safe so you can live peacefully."

"God is a builder. He is building a palace for you
in heaven so you can live with him someday."

"But do you know what God's favorite job is?
He is your Daddy in heaven. And he loves you.
He can hardly wait for the times you
bow your head and talk to him."

For Parents

God gave earthly fathers the honor of representing him to their children. Fathers also mirror God by working at jobs that provide for the family's needs. God's desire is that fathers also reflect him by placing their highest priority on loving their children. Although not every father does this, there are many who do. However, even the best father unintentionally makes mistakes that hurt his children. By teaching your child that God is our heavenly Father, and helping him or her begin to understand how very much God loves us, you can help heal that hurt.

Read it together

As you read through the book, pause briefly on each page to talk about the earthly counterpart to each job depicted, explaining how very important that job is.

Talk it over

Ask for your child's thoughts about which job is the most important or special. Does he or she agree that no job on earth is more important than that of being a daddy? Discuss the fact that a human daddy may get too busy or make a mistake, but God is a perfect heavenly Father. He loves his children very much and will always take care of them and stay close to them.

Taking action

Bow your heads together. Thank God that he is your good and loving Daddy in heaven. Then ask God, in Jesus' name, to help your child understand that God is *his or her* loving heavenly Father. Ask the Lord to help your child feel the depth of God's love. (For help in explaining the depth of God's love to your children, read Romans 8:35–36 and Ephesians 1:17–18. These verses speak of Christ's love, but Christ and God are one being— in complete agreement.)

Just for fun

Invite your child to come stand with you in front of a mirror. Look yourself directly in the eyes and say, "God is my perfect heavenly Father, and he loves me more than I can imagine!" Encourage your child to do the same.